4/09

DISCARDED

MAGGIE'S

MAGGIE'S STORY

Sheila O'Flanagan

BBC
LARGE
PRINT

First published in 1999 by
New Island Books
This Large Print edition published
2008 by BBC Audiobooks by
arrangement with
New Island Books

ISBN 978 1 405 62240 0

British Library Cataloguing in Publication Data available

Printed and bound in Great Britain by
CPI Antony Rowe, Chippenham, Wiltshire

Chapter One

The kitchen door opened. Tom strode into the room. He sat down on the chair and stretched his legs out in front of him.

'What's for tea?' he asked.

Maggie turned to look at her twenty-year-old son. He was glancing through the paper, ignoring her.

She stirred the pot on the hob. 'Curry,' she said.

He looked up from the paper. 'What sort?'

'Chicken curry.'

'With fruit?'

'Yes.'

'Good,' said Tom in satisfaction. 'I'm starving.'

The kitchen door banged open again. This time it was Dan, her husband, who came in. He dropped his bag of tools on the kitchen floor and sat down at the table opposite

Tom.

'What's for tea?' he asked.

Maggie picked up the pot of rice and began to drain it.

'Curry,' she said.

'What sort?' asked Dan.

'Chicken,' answered Tom. 'With fruit.'

'Great.' Dan rubbed his hands together. 'I'm starving.'

Maggie went to the kitchen door.

'Diana!' she called. 'Your food is ready.'

'I'll be down in a minute,' shouted Diana. 'I'm just finishing something up here.'

'Finishing her nails,' said Dan. 'Or her face.'

'She's supposed to be doing her homework.' Maggie spooned some rice onto a plate. 'She'll never get her exams with the amount of work she does.'

'With the kind of body she has she might find a rich bloke.' Dan laughed. 'Take her off our hands.'

'She'll need one,' said Maggie sourly. 'She'll never get anywhere on her own.'

Diana walked into the kitchen. Her blonde hair swung around her carefully made-up face. Her nails were painted a dark brown.

'I thought you were supposed to be doing homework,' said Maggie as she slid a plate of curry in front of her sixteen-year-old daughter. 'Not spending the afternoon tarting yourself up.'

'I'm not tarting myself up,' said Diana. 'I'm going out with Faye and Dervla later.'

'Have you done your homework?' asked Maggie. 'I suppose I have to remind you that your exams are only three months away?'

'Of course I've done my homework.' Diana mixed the curry sauce and the rice together. 'I do nothing but bloody homework. And what good is it going to do me? I don't want to go to college. I just want to get a job.'

'You need qualifications for every job,' said Maggie.

'Get off my case, will you?' snapped Diana. 'I know what I want out of life. And I don't need you nagging me all the time.'

Maggie pursed her lips and sat down.

Dan and Tom exchanged glances.

'Are you going out later?' Dan asked Tom.

'I'm meeting Peter. We're going to the Leisureplex.'

Maggie pushed her food around on her plate. She wasn't hungry.

'John Murphy asked me to drop around later,' Dan told her. 'He wants me to look at his engine.'

'Why couldn't he have brought it to the garage like anyone else?' asked Maggie.

'Because he doesn't get in until late,' explained Dan. 'And he's my friend, Maggie. I'll take a look at the engine and we'll probably go and have a drink.'

'Will you be late?' she asked.

Dan shrugged. 'I wouldn't say so. Just one drink—I'll be driving after all.'

She was silent. She watched them all as she ate.

Dan was still a good-looking man despite his forty-five years and greying hair. He had brown eyes that twinkled when he was happy, which was most of the time. Dan was one of those people who got on with everyone. He was happy to help out whenever he could and he never minded dropping around to a friend's house to have a look at a car, or give them advice on anything mechanical. Dan had worked all his life in garages. He was car-mad. There was nothing he liked more than being up to his arms in engine oil.

Tom was her eldest child. He worked in a DIY superstore. Tom, like Dan, was good at practical things, especially anything to do with the house. Tom had laid the patio at the back of the house last year and it couldn't have been done more professionally.

Diana had finished eating and was reading the magazine she'd brought to the table with her. Every time she looked at Diana, Maggie wondered where her daughter had got her looks. She was stunning. Tall, like Dan, and with the same huge brown eyes. Most people commented on how unusual it was to have brown eyes and fair hair. They wondered if blonde was her natural colour. But it was. She got it from her grandmother, Maggie's mother.

Diana wasn't interested in anything other than having a good time. Maggie worried about her constantly.

Dan ate the last of his curry and got up from the table.

'I'm going to put my feet up for a few minutes,' he said. 'Watch the

6

telly.'

'Me too.' Tom pushed his empty plate away. 'Any chance of a cup of tea, Mam?'

'I'll bring it into you,' Maggie said.

'Thanks.' Tom grinned at her.

Diana closed her magazine. 'I'm going up to change,' she said. 'I told Dervla I'd call around at half-seven.'

Tom looked at his watch. 'It's seven now,' he said. 'You'll never make it on time. It takes you at least an hour to decide what to wear!'

'Ha, ha, very funny.' Diana made a face at him.

'It improves you!' Tom laughed.

'Sod off,' she said.

'Please.' Maggie looked from one to the other. 'I'm not in form for your bickering tonight.'

'We're not bickering,' said Tom.

'Whatever,' said Maggie tiredly. 'I'm not in form for it, that's all.'

Tom went into the living-room while Diana stomped upstairs. Maggie poured boiling water into the teapot.

Sometimes she felt as though she didn't know her children any more. Or Dan either, come to that. They all seemed to live different lives and she didn't know whether she was part of them.

She sighed as she poured tea into the big blue mugs that Dan and Tom both liked. She was forty-three years old and she sometimes felt as though life had passed her by.

Chapter Two

Maggie didn't sleep well that night.

Dan had gone to look at John's car and it was eleven by the time he got home. She'd made him another cup of tea and he'd watched Sky News on the TV. Tom had come home at midnight. Diana had been about five minutes behind him.

Maggie had spoken sharply to Diana, who was supposed to be home by eleven on week nights. But Diana had just sighed deeply and gone to her room.

Maggie had lain in bed and listened to Dan snoring gently. She'd worried about Diana and about Tom too. She knew that he sometimes found the DIY superstore boring. She was afraid he might just chuck it in without another job to go to.

'Don't fuss,' he told her once. 'I know what I'm doing.'

But she couldn't help fussing. And worrying. For as long as she could remember, Maggie had worried about them. She supposed that, when it came to your children, you never stopped. She wanted everything to be easy for them. Even though, in her experience, nothing ever was.

She let Dan get up before her the next morning. Most mornings she was the first one to get up, but today she decided to lie on. They weren't helpless in the mornings, she thought as she listened to them getting ready. Of course, they hardly bothered with breakfast. Tom would grab a slice of bread and a cup of tea. Dan usually had a bowl of cereal. But they didn't linger over breakfast. Dan would drop Tom off at the DIY store. Then he'd drive to the garage.

When the front door slammed closed, Maggie got up. She rapped on the bedroom door.

'Diana! It's time to get up.'

There was no answer. Maggie pushed the door open. Diana was asleep. The sheets were tangled around her. She went over and shook her daughter.

'It's time to get up.'

Diana groaned and burrowed deeper beneath the sheets.

'You'll be late for school.'

'Go away,' mumbled Diana. 'I'm sick.'

'You certainly are not!' Maggie pulled the sheets off the bed. 'Come on, get up.'

'Oh, Mam!' Diana sat up and stared at her mother. Her hair tumbled around her shoulders. 'I'm so tired.'

'I'm not surprised,' said Maggie. 'How many times have I told you? Eleven on week nights.'

Diana shrugged. 'Everyone else stays out late.'

'I don't care what everyone else does,' said Maggie. 'And you'll be late for school.'

'It's only crummy Maths this morning,' said Diana. 'I won't miss much.'

'That's not the point,' said Maggie.

'I hate school.' Diana pulled on her dressing-gown. 'There's nothing they can tell me that I don't know already.'

Maggie stood under the shower while Diana drank black coffee for breakfast. She didn't like being in the kitchen at the same time as Diana in the morning. Not with 98FM blaring so loudly. Maggie had liked rock music when she was younger. But not this early in the day. She liked peace and quiet at eight o'clock in the morning.

'I'm off!' shouted Diana.

'Have a good day!' called Maggie as she rubbed shampoo into her hair.

*　　　*　　　*

Maggie worked for the Central

Statistics Office, or the CSO, as they called it. It was a part-time job. She interviewed people for the surveys that the office carried out. Maggie liked the job because it meant meeting people. Although she had a sore shoulder from the weight of the computer that she needed to carry with her. Some people looked worried when she switched on the computer. They'd ask her if she was recording information about them. If there'd be somebody around to check up on them. Maggie always assured them that the survey was completely confidential. Nobody could access anything, she'd tell them.

'But what about your children?' a harassed-looking mother once asked. 'They can probably access anything. I know mine can. Put him in front of a computer screen and the next thing you know he's talking to people in Albania.'

Maggie laughed. 'Not mine. They

can play games, that's all.'

'Oh, games!' The woman had snorted. 'Mine are worse on games. Mortal Kombat, Tomb Raider, Formula One—they play them all.'

'It could be worse.' Maggie laughed.

Of course, not everyone was chatty. Some people told her to sod off. Some just slammed the door in her face. But at least she met lots of different people. Maggie liked people.

She looked at her watch and booted up the computer. Time to go.

*　　　*　　　*

Maggie lived in Coolock and the area she covered for her interviews was around Fairview. She caught the bus on the Malahide Road. The worst of the morning traffic-jam was over now and the bus sailed down the quality bus corridor towards the city. Dan hated the quality bus corridor. He

14

said that it made driving on the Malahide Road almost impossible. And he had to drive to work because he took all his tools in the car with him. Maggie was supposed to have the use of a car for her job. Dan told her she could have his. She could catch the bus to the garage and take the car. But that didn't make any sense. Besides, Maggie didn't like driving Dan's Honda Prelude. She wasn't a very confident driver. She'd had some lessons, years ago, but she hadn't had time to finish the course. So she had never passed her driving test. Really, if she drove Dan's car, she'd need to stick L-plates on the windows. And she didn't want to do that. Although it would be nice to have a car of her own. It was a dream of Maggie's. To be able to drive her own car.

She'd asked Dan to teach her once. It was hopeless. Every time she stalled the car or made any mistake, she'd hear a deep intake of breath from her husband.

'It's OK,' she'd say angrily. 'I haven't crashed.'

'You're bloody going to!' he'd reply.

She stopped taking lessons from Dan. It wasn't worth the price of their marriage.

She pressed the bell and the bus slowed down. Maggie slung the computer in its carrying case over her shoulder and winced. But it was worth it just to earn her own money. Besides, it was money they needed. It was all very well for Tom to hand her something every week, but he didn't earn that much himself. And he ate more than the money he gave her!

As for Diana. Maggie sighed as she thought of her beautiful but lazy daughter. Diana said that she didn't have time for work because she was studying. Diana could easily work on Saturdays. There were plenty of part-time jobs available. But Diana went shopping on Saturdays. And she would ask Maggie for the money.

'Ah, go on Mam,' she'd say, turning her soft brown eyes to Maggie. 'Just a loan. That's all.'

It was always just a loan with Diana. Maggie wondered if she'd ever pay her back. She'd tried to teach Diana the value of money but she knew that she'd failed.

*   *   *

Her first interview was at a red-brick, terraced house. This was the second time Maggie had interviewed the resident here. As interviewers, they called to houses a number of times so that they could see how people's lives had changed.

A young girl lived in Number 23. With her boyfriend, remembered Maggie, as she walked up the path. The girl was a writer. Her boyfriend worked in a pub in Sutton.

Maggie rang the bell.

'Oh, it's you again.' The girl

pushed her hair out of her eyes. 'I didn't think you'd be back.'

'I'm afraid I've some more questions to ask,' said Maggie. 'Can you answer them?'

The girl sighed. 'I suppose so. I'm supposed to be working. Still –' she grinned at Maggie, 'any excuse to bunk off for a while.'

Maggie followed her into the yellow and blue kitchen. It was the brightest kitchen she'd ever seen. She compared it with her own—green and white. She'd liked her kitchen until she saw Flora's.

The girl's name was Flora. Maggie had looked out for a book by Flora but had never seen one.

There was a laptop computer on the kitchen table. It was surrounded by a pile of paper.

'If it's a bad time I can come back,' said Maggie.

'No, it's OK. Would you like coffee?' Flora was already filling the kettle.

'Thanks,' said Maggie, even though she didn't really want anything.

'OK.' Flora sat down beside her. 'What do you need to know now?'

'Same sort of thing.' Maggie opened her laptop computer. 'Do you work?'

Flora grinned. 'Yes.'

'Last week, did you work for payment or profit?'

Flora sighed. 'If you could call my royalties payment! And if you can call ripping up twenty pages work—then yes.'

Maggie smiled and keyed in the answer.

'Have you changed jobs since last time I called? That was three months ago, Flora.'

'No,' Flora said. 'Though sometimes I wish I did something different. But I'm still trying to write.'

Maggie asked her some more questions, which Flora answered as helpfully as she could.

'So how is the book coming along?'

Maggie shut down her laptop.

'I'm stuck,' said Flora. 'I keep having to change things.'

'Why are you stuck?'

'Because the heroine is a silly cow,' Flora told her. 'She's such a wimp! I don't know why I ever thought of her.'

Maggie laughed. 'I looked for a book by you,' she said. 'But I didn't see one.'

Flora smiled. 'That's because they're not under my name. My pen-name is Tamara Brook.'

'My goodness!' Maggie stared at her. 'I have seen books by you. I didn't realise you were Tamara Brook. It's a posh name!'

'It's supposed to sound romantic,' Flora told her. 'That's what I write, Maggie. Romantic novels.'

'I haven't read any,' admitted Maggie. 'Have you written many?'

'This is my fourth,' said Flora.

'I don't have time to read any more,' said Maggie. 'I used to. I used to read romances. And thrillers. Just about anything. But now, it's different.'

'Why?' asked Flora.

'Because of the family,' said Maggie. 'With a husband and two teenagers—even if one is working—there's just so much to do all the time.'

'You should keep some time for yourself,' said Flora. 'You deserve time to yourself.'

'Easier said than done.'

Flora smiled. She stood up and took a book off the shelf behind her. 'Here,' she said. 'This is the first one I wrote.'

Maggie looked at it. It was called *A Crazy Heart*. The cover showed a very dark, rugged-looking man glaring at a fair-haired woman.

'It's very thick,' said Maggie. She turned it over. 'What's it about?'

'What do you think?' Flora laughed. 'It's a romance, Maggie.'

'I'll bring it back next time,'

promised Maggie.

'Don't be silly,' said Flora. 'It's a present. Look—I'll sign it for you.' She picked up a pen and signed it 'Tamara Brook'.

Maggie stared at it. 'Doesn't it feel odd signing someone else's name?'

'Not to me,' said Flora. 'When I'm writing romances I think of myself as Tamara Brook. I'm a completely different person.'

'How are you different?' Maggie was curious.

'When I'm Tamara, I *am* romantic,' explained Flora. 'I go weak at the knees when I see tall, dark, handsome men! I think romantic thoughts. When I'm me, I'm worrying about the fact that I have a leak in the roof. And that my car is on its last legs.'

Maggie laughed. 'I wouldn't mind being two people.'

'It's easy,' said Flora. 'You just have to practise.'

'I will,' said Maggie. She zipped the

computer into its bag. 'I'd better get going. I've stayed far too long.'

'I didn't mind,' confessed Flora. 'I was looking for an excuse to take a break.'

Maggie waved goodbye and went to her next house. It was a few doors down. The elderly lady there didn't have time for a chat. She was going to her bridge class soon. So Maggie was finished much quicker.

Chapter Three

She started to read the book on the bus. The main character was a girl called Lisa. Lisa was tall and beautiful. She had perfect skin. She had a perfect figure. She also had a perfect boyfriend, Luke. They worked in the same company.

Maggie sighed as she thought of Lisa. She touched her own brown hair which needed to be cut. Lisa wouldn't step outside the house with her hair in a mess. Once, Maggie had been like that too. Now she hardly noticed how she looked.

The bus pulled up at Maggie's stop. She closed the book and jumped off.

It was starting to rain. She walked as quickly as she could. But she was still very wet by the time she opened the front door.

She made herself a cup of tea and

looked at Flora's book again. She really wanted to read some more. She was interested in Lisa and Luke. But the washing needed to be done. She couldn't believe how much dirty laundry there was in the house. Of course, Dan's job meant his clothes got dirty easily. Tom just threw things into the wash whenever he felt like it. And Diana! Maggie didn't know how Diana managed to have so many tops to wash.

She brought the laundry basket downstairs. She loaded the washing-machine with the forty-degree wash. There were still loads of clothes left. Tom had played soccer during the week and his kit was at the bottom of the basket. Maggie made a face as she looked at his white shorts. They were caked with mud. So were his socks. And his jersey was filthy.

She switched on the machine. There was still the ironing to do. When she finished that, she'd read some more.

She was on the last shirt when the front door opened. Diana walked into the living-room.

'You're home early,' said Maggie.

'I didn't feel well,' said Diana.

Maggie looked at her. 'What's the matter?'

'I've a headache.'

'I hope it's not a hangover.'

'Mam!' But Diana hung her head.

'You're sixteen years old,' said Maggie. 'Cop on to yourself, girl.'

'I am copped on,' said Diana.

'No you're not.' Maggie switched off the iron. 'All you think about is how you look. And boys. You don't care about school or your exams.'

'It's boring,' said Diana. 'I don't need to know half of it.'

'I know,' said Maggie. 'But when you're looking for a job—'

Diana laughed. 'I'm going to find myself a rich husband,' she told Maggie. 'I won't need a job.'

'Yes you will,' Maggie said. 'And—'

'Oh, Mam, give me a break!'

Diana walked out of the room and up to her bedroom, slammed her door behind her.

Maggie was stupid, Diana thought. She'd married Dan too soon. They'd been young and madly in love. Diana loved her father. But she thought Maggie should have played the field a bit before marrying him.

Maggie folded the last shirt and put the ironing board away. She looked at her watch. It was nearly five o'clock. Soon, she'd start the dinner. But she'd read a bit of the book first.

Things weren't going well for Lisa. She'd just found out that Luke was two-timing her. He was seeing another girl in the company. Lisa was shocked and hurt when she found out.

'I love both of you,' Luke told Lisa. 'I can't help it.'

'You have to choose,' Lisa said. And Luke chose the other girl,

Karen.

Why? wondered Maggie. Lisa was a nice character. Even if she was too beautiful to be true.

She glanced up at the clock. Half-past five! She closed the book quickly. It was time to make the dinner. Tom and Dan would be home soon. They weren't the kind of men who liked waiting for their food.

*   *   *

She slid the pork chops under the grill. Diana pushed open the kitchen door. She sat down at the table.

'What's for tea?' she asked.

'I thought you were sick,' said Maggie.

'I was,' Diana told her. 'But I feel much better now.'

'Really?'

'Yes, really.'

Maggie put the salt and pepper on the table. 'Pork chops,' she said.

Diana made a face. 'I don't like

pork chops.'

'Like it or lump it,' snapped Maggie.

Diana sighed and pushed her hair out of her eyes.

Maggie watched her daughter. Diana was a little bit like Lisa in the book, she thought. Blonde and beautiful, but wanting everything her own way. Maybe that was why Luke had dumped Lisa.

She turned the chops over. The door opened and Tom came in.

'What's for tea?' he asked.

'Pork chops,' said Diana.

'I hope there's loads,' said Tom. 'I'm starving.'

Maggie emptied a tin of beans into a pot and began to heat them up.

Dan arrived home.

'What's for tea?' he asked.

'Pork chops,' said Tom and Diana together. They started to laugh.

Maggie stirred the beans. No one had bothered to ask her about her day. They never bothered. They just expected her to do their washing and cook their meals. She was sick of them. She'd been married for twenty-two years. She was sick of washing and of cooking. And of looking after people who should be able to look after themselves.

After tea she sat on the sofa and read her book.

'What's that?' asked Dan. He was playing soccer on the Sony Playstation. Tom had gone out. Diana was in her room. She said she was doing homework. But Maggie could smell nail varnish.

'A book,' said Maggie.

'What book?' asked Dan.

She held it out to him.

'*A Crazy Heart*,' he read. He laughed. 'Sounds stupid.'

'It's not stupid,' said Maggie. 'It's good.'

'What are you doing buying books?' asked Dan. 'You don't read books.'

'I used to,' Maggie told him. 'And I didn't buy this. One of the people I interview gave it to me. She's the author.'

'Really?' Dan looked surprised. 'Is she rich? Is she famous?'

'I've heard of her,' said Maggie. 'She lives in Fairview. It's not a very big house. So she can't be that rich.'

'I thought they all made a fortune,' said Dan.

Maggie shrugged. 'I didn't ask her.'

'It's a stupid name,' said Dan.

'What?'

'Tamara Brook.'

'It's her pen-name,' explained Maggie. 'Her real name is Flora O'Brien.'

Dan laughed. 'I suppose she thinks Tamara Brook sounds better.'

'It's more romantic,' said Maggie.

'Where are you going, with romance?' Dan laughed again. 'After twenty-two years of being married! Romance is for kids.'

'Is it?' asked Maggie.

'Yes,' said Dan.

Maggie returned to her book. Lisa

left the company and got herself a new job. Maggie wasn't surprised at that. The new company was bigger than the old one. Lisa worked hard. The boss liked her. Maggie hoped he wouldn't make a pass at her! He was too old.

'Are you listening to me?'

Maggie looked up from the book.

'It's time for bed,' said Dan. 'It's eleven o'clock.'

'Just let me finish this chapter,' said Maggie.

'You haven't taken your nose out of it all night,' said Dan. 'Give it a break, Maggie.'

'I'll be up soon,' she told him. 'You go ahead.'

Lisa was sent to work in New York by the new company. While she was there she met a man. Rob Harris. He asked her out. He sounded gorgeous. He had black hair and blue eyes. He wore expensive suits. Lisa liked him, but she was still unhappy about breaking up with Luke. She couldn't get Luke out of her mind.

'Forget him,' said Maggie again. But this time she said it out loud.

Dan opened the living-room door.

'It's nearly one o'clock,' he said. 'I can't sleep without you beside me, Maggie. And I'm tired. So come to bed.'

'Oh, OK.' She sighed and closed the book. She'd try to finish it tomorrow.

Chapter Four

It was raining hard the next day. Maggie hoped the bus would be along quickly. Her feet were getting wet. The computer was heavy. She didn't feel like doing any interviews.

The man on River Road offered her a cup of tea. His name was Chris Casey. He was a manager at a nearby factory and worked different shifts. He'd just finished one.

'You're lucky,' he told her. 'Another ten minutes and I would have been asleep.'

'I don't want to keep you up,' she said. 'Forget the tea.'

'Ah, no.' He filled the kettle. 'I like having someone to talk to. Someone different.'

The first time she'd interviewed him, Maggie had asked details about his life. She knew that he was forty-six. His wife had left him on his fortieth birthday. The children lived with her.

'I'm used to it now,' he'd told her. 'But it was a killer at first. I get to see the younger kids once a week. The older ones call around sometimes. It's not too bad.'

Maggie felt very sorry for him.

She stirred her tea. 'How are things?' she asked.

'Oh, not bad.' He smiled at her. He had a nice smile. 'Well, what do you want to ask me about today?'

She asked the usual questions and keyed in his answers.

'See you in three months,' she said.

'Take care, Maggie.' He smiled at her again. 'I like seeing you.'

She blushed.

'I do!' He grinned. 'You're a fine-looking woman.'

'Chris!'

'If you weren't married, I'd be keen on you myself.'

'Chris!'

He laughed. 'I like it when you

blush,' he told her. 'It makes you look very young.'

She couldn't help thinking about him on the way home. A man had paid her a compliment. And Chris was a decent man. A nice man.

She went into the bedroom and looked at herself in the mirror. She couldn't help comparing herself to Lisa in the book. Lisa was the kind of girl that men really wanted. Young and beautiful. Maggie just looked tired.

Dan had once told her she was beautiful. When she'd first gone out with him. He'd always been so nice to her then. But now she was just part of the furniture.

She picked up a brush and ran it through her hair. Maybe if she got it cut, Dan would think she was good-looking again. But Chris Casey thought she was good-looking anyway. The thought made her smile.

She did the rest of the day's house-work. Then she sat down with the book.

Lisa had been promoted again. She was doing really well. Loads of blokes fancied her and asked her out. Rob Harris sent her flowers every week. But she wasn't interested in men any more. Her career was more important to her now.

I wish I'd had a career, thought Maggie. I wish I'd done something more exciting with my life than marrying Dan. I wish I had something to show for it all. She began to read chapter thirty.

Lisa's new company was going to buy her old one. And Lisa was now the personnel manager. She was going to make decisions about who was to stay and who was to go. She'd be in a position to fire Luke. The bastard who'd dumped her.

Go for it, Lisa, thought Maggie. 'Show him who's boss!' she said out loud, just as the front door opened.

Diana walked in.

'What are you doing?' she asked Maggie.

'What does it look like?'

'Reading a book,' said Diana.

'Exactly,' said Maggie.

'But why aren't you making the tea?'

'There's plenty of time,' said Maggie. 'You're only just in.'

'No, there's not,' said Diana. 'It's nearly six. I stayed in Carol's for a while after school.'

Maggie gasped and looked at the clock.

'Dad and Tom will be mad if they don't get any tea,' said Diana.

'I know,' said Maggie.

'You'd better get a move on,' said Diana.

Maggie closed the book.

'They should do it themselves,' she said.

Diana laughed. 'Can you see them?'

'No.' Maggie stood up. 'At least, I can see them making a mess of it. Same way as you'd make a mess of it.' She glanced at Diana.

'I'm hopeless at cooking,' said Diana. 'It's not my fault.'

'You're lazy about it,' said Maggie. 'You know how, you just don't bother. You're as bad as them. You expect me to wait on you hand and foot.'

'No I don't.' Diana shook her head. 'I make my own snacks, don't I?'

'Big deal,' said Maggie. 'A toasted cheese sandwich.'

'It's better than nothing at all.' Diana followed her into the kitchen.

'What's for tea?' she asked.

'Burgers and chips,' said Maggie. 'It's too late for anything else.'

'You were really stuck into that book.' Diana filled the kettle. 'What's it about?'

'It's called *A Crazy Heart*,' Maggie told her. 'And I know the author.'

'Do you?' Diana looked surprised.

'She lives in Fairview,' said Maggie. 'She signed it for me.'

39

'Is it any good?' asked Diana.

'It's interesting,' said Maggie. 'It's about a girl who gets dumped by her boyfriend. But then she's in a position where she can fire him from his job.'

Diana grinned. 'I like that! That sounds good.'

Maggie smiled. 'I know. And she is a lovely looking girl too.'

'Why did the boyfriend dump her?' asked Diana.

'He started going out with someone else,' Maggie told her. 'He didn't want to be tied down to one person. So he started going out with someone else in the office.'

'The shit,' said Diana.

'Mind your language,' said Maggie.

'Sorry,' said Diana.

'Anyway, I'm dying to see whether she'll fire him or not.'

'Do you think she will?'

'I don't know,' said Maggie. 'She's trying to be tough. But she's a softie at heart. She might let him walk all over her.'

She shook oven chips onto a baking tray.

'Would you have liked a job?' asked Diana.

'I have a job,' said Maggie. 'Looking after you. And the CSO!'

'A real job. Nine to five. Every day.'

'I only have time for the CSO,' Maggie told her.

'But if you didn't have to look after us,' said Diana. 'Do you ever wish you hadn't married Dad? Done something else instead?'

'I wish lots of things,' said Maggie. 'But I never wish I hadn't had my children.'

And that was true. No matter what. She loved the children. Even if they drove her mad sometimes.

Chapter Five

Dan was just getting out of the car as Tom arrived into the driveway.

'Hi, Dad,' said Tom. 'How are things?'

'Not bad.' Dan opened the boot and took out his tools. 'How about you?'

'I hate that bloody place,' said Tom. 'The manager is a complete pain. He's as thick as a plank too. I could do the job better myself.'

'At least it brings in the money,' said Dan.

'I know.' Tom opened the hall door. 'And with the overtime and everything it's not bad. It's just that I'd prefer to be doing something else.'

'Like what?' asked Dan.

'I'm not sure.' Tom sighed. 'I like the selling part. I like when people ask me about stuff. I can always give the right answer. Or help them out. I'd like a place of my own. One day.'

'With luck.' Dan pushed open the kitchen door. 'Hi, Maggie.'

She turned around. 'It'll be ready in a minute.'

Dan looked at the clock.

'I was late starting,' she added.

'She was reading a book,' said Diana who was sitting at the kitchen table.

'Not that bloody book again! For God's sake woman, I'm bloody starving. And you've been sitting around reading!'

Maggie shrugged. 'I've nearly finished it.'

'You could have written it, it's taking you so long to read it,' snapped Dan.

'It's a big book,' said Diana.

'Any chance of a cuppa while I'm waiting?' Dan plonked himself down at the table.

'No,' said Maggie.

'Here, I'll do it,' said Diana hastily.

43

'The kettle's boiled already.' She made a warning face at both Tom and Dan. 'Mam's a bit tired.'

'No, I'm not,' said Maggie.

'You look a bit pale,' said Tom.

'I don't,' Maggie told him.

'Ah, he's right,' said Dan. 'You're a bit tired, love. Run off your feet maybe? You should give up that CSO job. It's too much work.'

'I like it,' said Maggie. 'And it gives me money.'

'I give you money,' said Dan. 'Don't I give you enough?'

'Not always,' said Maggie.

Dan stared at her. 'I thought you did this job because you wanted to,' he said. 'It's not vital, is it? I mean, I'm earning enough, Maggie.'

'It's vital for me,' she said. 'And so that I can buy treats for the house without having to ask you.'

'But I don't mind you asking me,' said Dan.

'I mind,' said Maggie.

Dan and Tom glanced at each

44

other while Maggie took the chips out of the oven.

'I don't know what's wrong with her,' muttered Dan. 'She's been acting strange since the weekend.'

'Since she started reading that book,' said Tom.

Dan made a face. 'It's only some old romantic thing.'

Tom laughed. 'Well it's put her in a shocking mood, whatever it is!'

Maggie slid the burgers onto the plates. Tom was right, she thought. She'd been in a terrible mood all week. And she really didn't know why. She kept feeling sorry for herself. She didn't usually feel sorry for herself. And she kept worrying about her age. She didn't feel as though she was forty-three. And yet she had Dan and Tom and Diana to remind her. She felt restless. She wanted something exciting to happen in her life. Just once.

Maggie planned to finish the book that evening. Lisa had called Luke into her office. She'd looked at him and realised that he was worried about his job. She'd been able to see the fear in his eyes. He was afraid of her. Of the power that she now had over him. He knew that there were plenty of people who could do his job. Some of them might even be better qualified than him. And Lisa, the woman he'd dumped, was the person who'd decide on his future. He wished he hadn't dumped her. Karen was a lovely girl and he enjoyed going out with her. He wasn't going to marry her, though. But Lisa—maybe Lisa was the sort of girl he could marry. Should marry.

Maggie turned the pages quickly. Luke was trying to be nice to Lisa. To soft-soap her. He was being smarmy, thought Maggie. So that he would keep his job.

Lisa listened to him. If she fired him would it be out of spite? Or because there was someone better?

She wasn't sure. She'd have to think about it. She told Luke to close the door on his way out.

Maggie liked that bit. She imagined herself sitting behind a big desk and telling some bloke to close the door on the way out. It was a pleasant thought. She rubbed her eyes. She was tired. But there were only two chapters to go.

'Hey, Maggie?' Dan looked at her.

'What?'

'Fancy an early night?'

She was surprised. Dan never asked her if she fancied an early night!

'I'm reading,' she said.

'Come on, Mags,' said Dan. 'I'm in the mood! The kids are out.'

'Let me just finish this bit.'

'Forget it!' He got up and walked out of the room. A second later he put his head around the door. 'I'm going for a pint,' he said. 'I'll see you later.'

'OK,' said Maggie. 'See you later.'

In the end Lisa didn't fire Luke. She decided he should keep his job. She sat in her glass office and thought about how great her life was. And then she felt sad because she didn't have anyone to share it with.

There was a knock on the door and her assistant walked in. She was carrying a huge bouquet of flowers. Lisa was amazed. She couldn't guess who might be sending them.

Then Rob Harris walked in. He'd flown from New York to be with her. He told her she was the only woman in the world for him. And then he kissed her. In the office. Where people could see.

The ending was a bit corny, Maggie thought. Blokes didn't really do things like bring you flowers and tell you they loved you. Blokes expected you to believe that the fact that they lived with you was proof enough. Dan had never bought her flowers. Ever. Last year, for her birthday, he'd bought her a deep-fat fryer. Even though she always bought oven chips.

Chapter Six

On Saturday nights Dan and Maggie usually went out to The Dollymount House with some friends. Tony and Rita owned a lighting shop in Coolock.

'We've got some lovely new uplights in,' said Rita, as Tony handed her and Maggie their drinks. 'You could put one in the corner of the living-room. It'd look really well.'

'Maybe,' said Maggie.

'They're going like hot-cakes,' said Rita. 'Of course all the trendy young things are buying them.'

'Oh?'

'Yes. Especially the people living in the new apartments. They all think they're being different and stylish, but they're all buying the same stuff.'

Maggie smiled.

'We had a couple in this morning,' said Rita. 'Spent an absolute fortune on lighting. Kept kissing each other as they walked around the shop.'

'Thank God we've got past that!' Dan, who'd overheard the last sentence, butted in. 'I can't see me and Maggie kissing our way around a shop.'

'Sure, you don't kiss me at all!' blurted Maggie.

'No.' Dan laughed. 'We move straight into something far more interesting.'

But I'd like it if you kissed me, thought Maggie. If you were more romantic. If you didn't say things like 'Hey, Maggie, fancy an early night?' And if it was more exciting. She blushed. What a thing to be thinking now.

'Maggie?' Rita was looking at her. 'Is everything OK?'

*   *   *

'She's been acting a bit funny for a while,' said Dan to Tony as they stood at the bar. 'I don't know what it is.'

'She looks all right,' said Tony.

'It's nothing about how she looks,' said Dan. 'It's just—everything else. Like she's living somewhere else.'

'They all go like that sometimes,' said Tony. 'But they get over it. It's hormones.'

'You're probably right,' said Dan. He ordered pints for them both.

*   *   *

'How's Diana?' Rita asked Maggie. 'I saw her in the shopping centre this afternoon. She looked great.'

'She always looks great.' Maggie sipped her drink. 'Though she complains about her weight every day! I worry about her, though, Rita.'

'Why?' Rita looked surprised.

'Because she doesn't care about anything other than having a good time.'

'She's dead right,' said Rita. 'You

can spend too much time on everything else.'

'But she needs to get her exams,' protested Maggie.

'I know.' Rita smiled at her friend. 'And she will, Maggie. Honestly.'

'I wish I could believe that,' said Maggie.

'Believe it,' said Rita. 'Think about Jenny.'

Jenny was Rita's grown-up daughter.

'Remember how she was a complete tearaway when she was at school?' asked Rita. 'Now she's doing really well in the Corporation.'

'I'd love to see Diana safely in the Corpo,' said Maggie.

'Don't tie her down too quickly,' Rita told her. 'She's only sixteen, Maggie. She has to have some fun.'

'I don't have any fun,' snapped Maggie. 'I don't see why she should!'

'Maggie!' Rita looked at her in surprise. 'Is everything all right?'

Maggie sighed. 'Oh, I suppose so. I

53

don't know what's wrong with me, Rita. These last few weeks I just feel like my whole life has been such a waste.'

'Why would you feel like that?' asked Rita. 'Haven't you got two lovely children, a grand house and Dan?'

Maggie smiled a little. 'It sounds great when you put it like that. But I keep thinking of what I should have done with my life.'

'Like what?' asked Rita.

'I don't know,' said Maggie. 'That's the point. I always thought I'd get married and have kids and that's exactly what I've done. I just wish I'd done something more, that's all.'

'Like what?'

Maggie shrugged. 'I should have had more boyfriends. I only had one before Dan! I wish I'd had more romance in my life.'

'Romance!' Rita laughed. 'We're a bit old for that.'

'I am now,' said Maggie. 'I wasn't

before.'

Rita looked at her thoughtfully. 'You need a break,' she said. 'Are you and Dan going away for the summer?'

'Are you mad?' asked Maggie. 'You know how he is. He hates going abroad. He hates being outside of Dublin!'

'Why don't you have one of those little mini-breaks?' asked Rita. 'You know, a couple of nights in a hotel. At least that way you'd feel pampered. And that would be romantic.'

'To be honest, I feel like I need time away from everyone,' said Maggie. 'I need time for myself.'

'I know what you mean.' Rita gave Maggie a hug. 'If I get any good ideas, I'll let you know.'

*   *   *

'Maybe she's working too hard,' said Tony as he took another pint from

Dan. 'Maybe she needs a holiday.'

'How can she be working too hard?' asked Dan. 'The CSO job is only part-time. I know she has to go out some evenings, but it's not like my job. It's not a ten-hour day. Or a twelve-hour day. Besides, she likes it. She's told me often enough. It's the one way she gets to meet new people.'

'Perhaps it's the people she's meeting!' Tony laughed. 'Maybe they're giving her ideas.'

Dan sighed. 'I hope not! Though she got a book from one of them. A love story, I think. Maybe that's what's wrong. She's reading some drivel about true love and stuff.'

'You can show her a thing or two in that department!' Tony laughed again. And so did Dan. But he frowned too.

*   *   *

Maggie rubbed cleanser into her

face.

'Don't bother with that,' said Dan. 'Come to bed, Maggie.'

'You're supposed to take make-up off every night,' said Maggie.

'What will happen if you don't?' asked Dan.

'I'm not sure.' Maggie wiped her face. 'But I've always done this.'

'Come on, Maggie,' he said. 'Hurry up.'

'I have to clean my teeth,' she told him.

He sighed and closed his eyes. He could hear the buzz of the electric toothbrush. He'd had four pints and he was sleepy. He wished Maggie would hurry up. He didn't want to fall asleep before she came back. He wanted to be loving to her. Show her that he cared.

Maggie stood in front of the bathroom mirror. Her eyes were a little bit red. That was from the smoke in the pub. She picked up her tweezers and plucked a few stray hairs from her eyebrows.

She was being silly, she thought. She was just going through a phase of being unhappy. Nobody could be happy with their life all of the time. Dan probably felt unhappy too sometimes. And she never even noticed. She was too caught up in herself.

She sprayed herself with Musk from the Body Shop. Diana had bought it for her the time that Dan had bought the deep-fat fryer.

Dan was snoring gently. Maggie stood at the side of the bed and watched him. She slid into bed beside him. He grunted and rolled over onto his side. Maggie turned out the bedside light. She put her arm around him. But he didn't wake up.

Chapter Seven

Maggie put six tins of baked beans into her shopping trolley. She always did her shopping on Monday mornings. The shop was quieter then.

She looked at her list. Tom wanted Gillette blades. She found them and threw them into the trolley. Diana wanted her to buy a new low-fat spread. And some low-calorie pasta sauce. Maggie shook her head. She would have to talk to Diana about all this low-fat stuff. She wasn't certain it was as good for you as Diana thought.

'Hello, Maggie.'

She turned around in surprise. It took her a moment to recognise the man beside her. It was Chris Casey. The man she interviewed who was separated from his wife and children.

'Hello Mr Casey,' she said. 'I didn't

know you did your shopping here.'

'Sometimes,' he said. He looked at her trolley. 'Stocking up?'

She smiled. 'I do a big shop on Monday mornings.'

He looked at his own trolley. It was only a third full.

'I'm supposed to be stocking up too,' he said. 'The children will be staying with me this weekend.'

'Are you looking forward to it?' she asked.

'Yes and no,' said Chris. 'I want them to stay, but I'm nervous. They've never stayed over before.'

'Why are they staying?' asked Maggie.

'Well, June—that's my wife—is going on a short holiday. And the younger kids need to be looked after. Mick is my eldest, but he's over in London at the moment. Tina is next. She's seventeen. But she's at school until after they get back and I don't want them at home on their own.'

Maggie tried to remember what

he'd said about his children. 'So it's the three youngest?'

He beamed. 'Yes. Emma and Paula, the twins—they're thirteen. And Alan. He's nine.'

'Do you still miss them?' asked Maggie. 'Because they're not there all the time?'

'Of course,' said Chris. He looked at his watch. 'Are you busy?' he asked.

'Not really,' said Maggie.

'Would you mind helping me with the shopping? I'm used to shopping for one. Not four.'

'Of course.' She smiled at him. 'I'm good at shopping!'

When they'd finished, Chris treated her to coffee and cake in the café.

'Thanks,' he said. 'Without you, I would have got all sorts of useless stuff.'

'No, you wouldn't,' said Maggie.

'I would.' He smiled at her. 'By the way, you've got cream on your chin.'

'I haven't!' She rubbed at it.

'It's gone now,' said Chris.

'Thanks.'

'I used to come here with June,' said Chris suddenly.

'Did you?'

'She'd do the shopping and we'd always have coffee here.'

'Why didn't you do the shopping?' asked Maggie.

'Come on, Maggie. You've seen me. I'm hopeless.'

'No, you're not.' She smiled at him.

'Was it hard?' she asked. 'When your wife left?'

Chris finished his coffee. 'Yes,' he said. 'I couldn't believe it at first. I thought she'd come back. But she didn't. And neither did the kids.'

'Why did she leave?' asked Maggie.

'I don't know.' Chris stared into the distance. 'At least—she said it was because I worked so hard. She said she never saw me. She said she wanted something else from life.'

Maggie shivered. The things June

had said sounded like how she felt. There were days when she saw Dan for only a couple of minutes. There were days when it all seemed like such a slog.

'Didn't you talk about it?' she asked.

'I wasn't a good talker,' said Chris. 'And I didn't take her seriously. I should have.'

He smiled. Maggie smiled back at him. He was very nice, she thought. She couldn't believe he'd been a bad husband.

'How about you, Maggie?' he asked. 'How long are you married?'

'Twenty-two years,' she said.

'Well done,' said Chris. 'You're still together. And it's not easy. At first it is. But then there are responsibilities.'

Maggie made a face. 'My life is nothing but responsibilities.'

'What do you do for fun?' asked Chris.

'Fun?' She frowned. 'I don't know.'

'You don't know?'

'We go to the pub on Saturdays,' she said. 'With friends.'

'But for yourself, Maggie?' Chris asked. 'For you?'

She was silent. She couldn't believe that there was nothing. She must do something for fun. What sort of person was she?

'You've got lost,' said Chris. 'Lost in being a wife and mother. Lost looking after things. You've forgotten about you.'

'That's not true,' she said. 'These last few weeks I've been thinking about me all the time.'

'And?'

'And what?'

'Are you happy?'

She sighed. 'I don't know.'

Chris smiled at her. 'Why don't we have some fun today?'

'What?'

'A fun day, Maggie. For you.'

She looked worried. 'I don't think—'

'Just fun, Maggie. That's all.'

'I have the shopping to get home. I have to get a taxi. I don't drive.'

'I'll drop you and the shopping home,' said Chris.

It seemed wrong somehow. Yet the idea was nice. A day of fun for her.

'What would you like to do?' he asked.

'Do?'

'We'll do whatever you want.'

'I'd like to walk on the beach,' said Maggie. 'I haven't done that in ages. Or watch a movie. Or get my hair cut —and coloured! To paint my nails. To eat a box of chocolates.' She laughed. 'Silly things, aren't they?'

'Not at all,' said Chris. 'Come on, I'll drive you home and then we'll go to the beach.'

*   *   *

It wasn't a very good day for the beach. The wind came in from the sea. The waves were green and frothy. There weren't many people around. Maggie's hair blew across her face.

'I love it here!' cried Chris. 'I always have.'

'It's a shame to live so close and not come more often,' said Maggie.

'I come here every weekend,' said Chris. 'I love Dollymount. I brought my first girlfriend here!'

Maggie blushed. He laughed.

They walked for miles. Maggie's hands were cold.

'I'll warm them for you,' said Chris. 'Give them to me.'

She held out her hands. He put his own around them. She shivered.

'Still cold?'

'It's not the cold,' she said.

They stood together. Maggie thought he was going to kiss her. She felt very guilty.

'Come on,' said Chris. 'If we walk back quickly you'll warm up.'

It was warmer in the car.

'What now?' asked Chris.

'I don't mind.' Maggie looked at

her watch. It was only one o'clock. It seemed much later.

'The movies,' said Chris. 'You wanted to go to see a film.'

'I don't mind really,' said Maggie. 'Perhaps I should get home.'

'Day of fun,' said Chris. 'Come on.'

They went to the UCI in Coolock. Chris brought her to see *Enemy of the State*. Maggie liked Will Smith. Chris liked Gene Hackman. He bought the tickets even though she offered to pay.

So Maggie bought popcorn and sweets.

'I feel like a teenager,' she said.

She liked sitting beside Chris in the dark. Their arms were touching. Maggie wondered what she'd do if he put his arm around her. But he didn't.

'That was good,' she said when the movie was over.

'Yes, it was,' said Chris.

Maggie looked at her watch. 'I have to get home,' she said.

'Why?' asked Chris.

'Because Diana will be home. And I have to cook for Dan and Tom.'

'Let them do it themselves,' said Chris. 'Stay with me for a while.'

'I can't,' said Maggie.

He put his arm around her. 'Why not?'

She liked him holding her. It was comforting.

'Oh, Chris—' she sighed.

'I like you, Maggie,' he said. 'You're a decent woman.'

'And I should be at home with my family,' she told him.

'Are you sure?'

She looked up at him. 'No. But they're expecting me.'

'OK,' said Chris. He kissed her on the cheek. 'I'll leave you home.'

Chapter Eight

The kitchen door banged open.

'What's for tea?' asked Tom.

He sat down at the kitchen table and opened the newspaper.

'Hello, Mam,' said Maggie. 'How was your day? Any news? What's for tea? Can I help?'

Tom closed the paper and looked at her. 'Are you feeling all right?'

'Oh, fine,' she said. 'Just fine.'

'Only you sound a bit annoyed.'

'I am,' she said. 'Just for once it would be nice if you said something else when you came home.'

'What do you mean?'

'Something other than "What's for tea?"'

'It's a greeting,' said Tom. 'That's all. And I'm starving.'

Maggie banged a pot onto the hot-plate.

The door opened and Dan walked

in. Tom looked at him in warning but Dan didn't notice.

'Hello, Maggie. What's for tea?'

Maggie banged another pot on the hot-plate. Dan looked at her in surprise.

'What's the matter?' he asked.

'What's for tea! That's the matter!'

Dan stared at her.

'Mam's tired of us asking what's for tea,' Tom explained. 'She wants us to ask something else instead.'

'Like what?' asked Dan.

'For God's sake!' Maggie turned to him. 'All I want is someone to realise that I have a life too. And it isn't just making your bloody tea!'

'I never said it was.'

'You act like it is,' she snapped. 'The both of you!'

Tom and Dan looked at each other.

'You think the only thing I think about all day is your bloody teas!' said Maggie. 'That I get up in the morning and I think about what I'm going to cook. That all the time I'm making beds I'm thinking about what to cook. That when I'm shopping I'm thinking about what to cook. Well, I don't bloody think about it all the time! Or even half of the time!'

'I didn't think you did,' said Dan.

'Well what do you think I do all day?' she asked.

'I don't know.' He looked puzzled. 'Read the paper? Go for a walk? Clean the house? Do some interviews?'

She rubbed her eyes. 'You see—you don't care.'

'Of course I care,' said Dan. 'But I don't know what's bothering you.'

'I'd just like someone to come in and ask me about my day,' said Maggie. 'That's all.'

'But I do ask you,' said Dan.

'No you don't,' said Maggie. 'You ask me if I've done things. If I've ironed your best shirt. If I've picked up your jacket from the cleaner's. If I've found the letter from the tax

71

people you've lost. That's the kind of thing you ask.'

'You're being silly,' said Dan.

Tom winced. He didn't think that was a good thing to say. Neither did Maggie.

'It's spaghetti bolognese for tea,' she said. 'The kettle has boiled. The pasta needs to be cooked. Do it yourself!'

She undid her apron and flung it onto the table. Then she walked out of the kitchen and banged the door behind her.

Tom and Dan stared at each other.

'What was all that about?' asked Dan.

'I haven't a clue,' said Tom.

'She was pretty mad,' said Dan. 'Maybe I should go up to her.'

'Maybe you should let her cool down.'

'You could be right.' Dan got up and looked at the pot. Maggie had left a handful of dry spaghetti beside it. 'Do I just pour water over this?'

Tom stood beside him. 'I think so. She usually kind of bends it into the pot.'

Dan picked up the spaghetti and put it into the empty pot. He pushed down on it and the strands broke. He looked surprised.

'Is that supposed to happen?' he asked.

'No,' said Tom. 'I told you. It bends.'

'Maybe I need the water in first,' said Dan.

'You're right!' Tom grinned at him. 'She puts the water in first.'

'Turn on the tap,' said Dan.

He held the pot under the cold tap while Tom ran the water. Then he tried to push the spaghetti into the pot again. It broke again.

'Ah, what's the matter with it?' he asked.

Tom shook his head. 'I don't know. I thought you were right about the water.'

At that moment, Diana walked in.

'What are you doing?' she asked.

'Making the tea,' said Dan. 'What does it look like?'

'Where's Mam?'

'Upstairs, I think.'

'What's she doing up there?'

'She was a bit upset.'

'About what?'

'Nothing,' said Tom. 'Hey, Diana, do you know how to cook this?'

'What is it?' she asked.

'Spaghetti.'

'What are you doing with it?'

'Putting it in water.'

'Cold water?' she asked.

Tom nodded.

Diana laughed. 'Even I know that it should be boiling water! Boiling water and a splash of oil. To stop it sticking.'

'Oh.' Dan and Tom looked embarrassed.

Diana laughed again. 'I'll go up and tell her,' she said, 'that you can't even cook spaghetti.'

'We can manage,' said Dan. 'And

you leave your mother alone. She isn't in the mood for you either.'

*   *   *

Maggie sat on the edge of the bed. She could hear the hum of their voices. But she couldn't hear what they were saying.

A tear rolled down her cheek. It had been so different today. With Chris Casey. He'd been kind and nice. He made her feel needed. But not in the way that Dan and Tom and Diana did. Not for cooking and cleaning. Even though she'd helped him with his shopping!

She touched her cheek where he'd kissed her. She felt as though everyone knew. As though her cheek was marked.

But nobody had noticed. Nobody knew that she'd had a different day today. A romantic day. With another man.

She rubbed her eyes. When she'd

married Dan she'd pictured them doing everything together. She'd imagined they would always love each other the way they did then.

She wondered if Dan still loved her. Or even if she still loved him.

Chapter Nine

Maggie pushed open the gate of Flora O'Brien's house. She walked up the path and knocked on the door.

'Oh, hello.' Flora looked at her in surprise. 'I didn't think you'd be back so soon.'

'I just came to say thanks for the book,' said Maggie.

'You're welcome,' Flora said. 'I hope you enjoyed it.'

'It was great,' said Maggie.

Flora smiled. 'I'm glad. I'm always very worried about that. I'm afraid people won't like them.'

'I couldn't put it down,' said Maggie. 'I loved it when Lisa had to interview Luke.'

'Do you want to come in for a minute?' asked Flora. 'Or are you in a hurry?'

'I'm doing interviews,' said Maggie.

'Oh, come on,' said Flora. 'You

know how it is. I always want a break!'

Maggie followed her into the kitchen. It was a mess. The blue and yellow wallpaper had gone and the walls were bare.

'Pat is decorating,' said Flora. 'That's why the place looks like a bomb hit it. And that's why I can't work. I hate it like this.'

'Why don't you get someone in?' asked Maggie.

Flora sighed. 'I can't afford it,' she said. 'The mortgage on this place is crazy. It's cheaper for Pat to do it.'

'Why are you doing it at all?' asked Maggie. 'I liked the blue and yellow.'

Flora blushed. 'It's my fault.'

'Why?'

'We were having a row. I threw a few things.'

'What sort of things?' asked Maggie.

'A cream cake. A bowl of strawberry mousse. A glass of wine. They all hit the wallpaper. It was destroyed.'

'Oh my God,' gasped Maggie. 'Were you mad?'

Flora shrugged. 'I can't help it. When I'm annoyed I throw things.'

'Couldn't you have just cleaned it up?'

'This was Pat's revenge,' said Flora. 'He said he'd do it up for me. I'd shouted that I hated him and I hated this house and I hated everything!'

'And do you?'

'Not at all.' Flora grinned. 'But I couldn't help it. I'd had a bad day. My hero is supposed to be a shit but he keeps doing nice things! I can't seem to write him as bad as I want.'

Maggie laughed. 'I thought you could make them do whatever you liked?'

'Not really.' Flora shook her head. 'The people in my books start to live their own lives. You can't stop them.'

'So you've created a bad person but he's not really so bad?'

'Yes,' said Flora. 'And he's costing me a fortune in decorating.'

'It would be simpler to get someone in,' Maggie said again. 'If you like I could ask my son about it. He's good at decorating. He works in a DIY store. He'd get this sorted in a couple of days.'

'Would he?'

'Yes,' said Maggie. 'And it wouldn't be too expensive. But it's up to you. Do you want me to get him to call?'

Flora nodded. 'I can't depend on Pat,' she said. 'And I need it to be tidy before I can work. It's impossible now.'

'Do you get bored here all day on your own?' asked Maggie. 'Especially when you can't write.'

'Not really. Two mornings I give writing classes. I do an afternoon show on the local radio on Fridays. I do some script writing for the soap they do on it too. And I do a weekly piece for a magazine. That brings in a regular income.'

'Don't you earn money from the books?'

'Not as much as you'd think,' said Flora. 'But one day, perhaps!'

'It sounds like a great life all the same,' said Maggie.

'Sometimes it is, sometimes it isn't,' said Flora.

Maggie sighed. 'Well, it's better than mine.'

'Why?'

'In the mornings I clean up. Then I do interviews. I go home and do some more house-work. Then I do interviews. Then I go home and cook for the family. And they don't bloody well appreciate it.'

Flora smiled at her. 'I'm sure they do.'

'It's a boring life,' said Maggie. 'Yours is interesting. And in your books everyone has an interesting life. None of them has a crummy job with the CSO.'

'I might give one of them a job there.' Flora looked thoughtful. 'One of them needs a part-time job. This might be just the thing.'

'Not really,' Maggie said.

'Why not?' asked Flora. 'You'll have to tell me about it, Maggie. Give me lots of info. So that I can write about it properly.'

'You're not serious?'

'Of course I am,' said Flora. 'It's ideal.' She grinned at Maggie. 'Why don't we fix a time? You can call back when you're not busy. And we can go through it all. You can tell me what you do every day.'

'Really?'

'Yes,' said Flora. 'And then you'll be in the book, Maggie!'

Maggie smiled. She liked that idea. Nobody else she knew was a character in a book. She agreed to come back in two days. She said goodbye to Flora and walked down the street.

'Hi, Maggie!'

She turned around. Chris Casey was standing on the other side of the road. She blushed.

'How are you?' he called.

'I'm OK.' She stood still.

He crossed the road.

'How are you?' she asked.

'I'm fine.' He smiled at her.

'And the kids?'

'They're fine too. They had plenty to eat and drink and it was good to have them stay with me. It felt like they were mine again.'

'That's good,' she said.

They were silent.

'I enjoyed the other day,' said Maggie. 'Thank you.'

'I'm glad,' said Chris.

They were silent again.

'I don't think we should do it again,' she said.

'Probably not,' said Chris.

'It's just –'

'It's OK, Maggie,' said Chris. 'I understand.' He smiled. 'It was just a day of fun. That's all.'

'Yes.' She nodded. 'That's all.'

'Maggie?'

'Yes?'

'Don't worry,' said Chris. 'I'm not

going to mess with your life.

Maggie sighed. 'I feel guilty about the day of fun!'

'Probably because you think you should have been with your husband. Like I should have been with June. But I left it too late, Maggie. Don't make the same mistake! You have a family still. And I think they love you. And you love them. You're lucky, Maggie.'

She smiled at him. 'I'll try to remember that.'

He smiled too. 'I enjoyed myself. I should get out more. You've made me see that. I just have to do it in future.'

'Yes,' said Maggie.

'I've got to go,' said Chris. 'I'll see you, Maggie.'

'See you, Chris.'

Am I lucky? wondered Maggie, as she sat on the bus. Is Chris right? Does Dan still love me? Even after twenty-two years?

Chapter Ten

The house was quiet. Maggie sat down at the table and backed up her CSO disks. When she'd finished, she looked around the kitchen. Tom had decorated it last year. It was pale green. He'd put up new presses for her too. In pine. With green handles. He'd do a good job for Flora. She knew he would.

She zipped the computer back in its bag. Then she went upstairs. She opened the door to Diana's room. By Diana's standards, it was tidy. At least all her dirty clothes were in the basket. Not on the floor like usual. And her clean clothes were in drawers. Or hanging up.

She looked at her watch. Time to start the tea. She opened the freezer and took out some chops.

Diana walked in just as she'd finished defrosting them.

'Hi,' she said. 'How are things?'

'OK,' said Maggie.

'Can I ask you something?'

'Yes, sure.'

'Do you think I'd be any good at fashion design?'

'Fashion design?' Maggie looked at her. 'What do you mean?'

'Designing clothes,' said Diana.

'You know enough about them,' said Maggie.

'I know that!' Diana grinned. 'And I wasn't bad at making them. But I lost interest. It's just that I think I might be getting interested again. What if I went to design college though?'

'Would you get enough points in your exams?' asked Maggie.

'Miss Murphy thinks so,' said Diana. 'She's encouraging me.'

'Well, so will I,' said Maggie. 'And I'm sure you'd be great at it.'

'Thanks.' Diana kissed her. 'Will you help me with my revision later?'

'We'll see,' said Maggie.

'Ah, go on,' said Diana. 'If it means I get a decent job.'

Maggie laughed. 'I suppose so.'

'Thanks,' said Diana again. 'Do you want me to peel a few spuds?'

The kitchen door banged open. Tom came in.

'How was your day?' he asked.

Maggie stared at him in surprise. 'What?'

'Your day?' asked Tom. 'How was it?'

'Fine,' she said. 'It was fine.'

He sniffed the air. 'Chops for tea?'

She smiled. 'Yes.'

'Good,' he said.

He filled the kettle and plugged it in. Then he sat down at the table and opened the newspaper.

Dan came in five minutes later.

'Evening all,' he said. He walked over to Maggie and kissed her on the cheek. 'How was your day?' he asked.

'For God's sake!' Maggie banged a spoon into the sink. 'Would you all stop asking me how my day was?'

They stared at her.

'I thought you wanted us to ask?' said Tom.

'Well, I do,' agreed Maggie. 'It's just a bit weird the way you're all doing it.'

'So you're mad at me if I ask and mad at me if I don't,' said Dan. 'I can't see how I can win in that situation.'

'You're supposed to ask and mean it,' said Maggie.

'I do mean it,' he said.

Maggie began to mash the potatoes.

'I'm not good at this stuff,' said Dan. 'But I do love you, Maggie. And I appreciate you.'

'Oh, really.' She mashed the potatoes a bit more.

'And I'm sorry if you think we don't care about you. We do.'

'I know,' she said.

'But we haven't been very good at showing it.'

'I know that too,' she said.

'But we want to show it,' said Dan.

'And we tried to think of a good way.'

'And what did you come up with?' asked Maggie. 'A maid for me?'

'Don't be mad,' said Dan. 'Not quite. Come with me.'

They trooped into the hall and out to the driveway. There was a car in the driveway. Not Dan's Honda Prelude, but a Ford Fiesta.

'It's for you,' said Dan. 'So you can get around a bit more. It's not new, of course. But it's in great nick. I've checked it myself.'

'And this is for you too.' Tom opened the door and handed her vouchers for driving lessons. 'We knew you wouldn't let Dan teach you.'

'And this way you'll be able to pick me up from places.' Diana beamed at her. 'So you won't have to worry about me.'

Maggie laughed. 'Is this car for me or for you?'

'It's for you,' said Dan. 'From all of us. With love.'

She stared at the car. Then at Dan. At Tom. And at Diana. They were beaming at her. She felt tears in her eyes. She loved them. And they loved her.

'Thanks,' she said. Her voice was shaky. 'Thanks a million.'

Dan put his arms around her and hugged her. Then he kissed her.

Dan was a good kisser. That was why she'd fallen for him in the first place.

'We'd better look after the tea,' said Diana. 'God knows how long they'll be out here.'

*   *   *

Maggie was sitting watching the TV when the doorbell rang. Nobody got up to answer it. They were all glued to the telly.

'Maggie Fagan,' said the man outside. 'These are for you.'

Maggie stared at the biggest bouquet of flowers she'd ever seen.

'Are you sure?' she asked.

'Certain.' The man smiled. 'Someone loves you.'

'To Maggie,' said the card. 'From Dan. With all my love.'

'Someone certainly does,' she said. She held the flowers to her. 'And I'm so lucky. I really am.'

Kc